Angelina Ballerina

and the
Art Fair

Based on the stories by Katharine Holabird
Based on the illustrations by Helen Craig

Ready-to-Read

Simon Spotlight
New York   London   Toronto   Sydney   New Delhi

SIMON SPOTLIGHT

An imprint of Simon & Schuster Children's Publishing Division

1230 Avenue of the Americas, New York, New York 10020

This Simon Spotlight edition August 2021

© 2021 Helen Craig Ltd. and Katharine Holabird. The Angelina Ballerina name and character and the dancing Angelina logo are trademarks of HIT Entertainment Limited, Katharine Holabird, and Helen Craig.

Illustrated by Mike Deas

SIMON SPOTLIGHT, READY-TO-READ, and colophon are registered trademarks of Simon & Schuster, Inc.

For information about special discounts for bulk purchases, please contact Simon & Schuster Special Sales at 1-866-506-1949 or business@simonandschuster.com.

Manufactured in the United States of America 0721 LAK

10 9 8 7 6 5 4 3 2 1

ISBN 978-1-5344-9511-1 (hc)

ISBN 978-1-5344-9510-4 (pbk)

ISBN 978-1-5344-9512-8 (ebook)

Angelina Ballerina
looked out of her window.

She was very excited.
She was going to make
a project for the
village art fair!

Her cousin Henry
was making a project too.

They decided to make their
art projects together.

Mrs. Mouseling helped them get started.

Angelina thought about
all the fun things she
could make from clay.

"I know!" she decided.
"I will make a dancer!"

Angelina practiced poses in front of the mirror.

Soon, she started
to mold the clay.

Angelina had fun
making her project!

Angelina was very happy
with her little dancer.

"Hooray, Angelina!"
Henry said.

Henry was working
on a painting.

He showed it to Angelina.
"This is me at the beach!"
Henry said proudly.

"I love to play
in the waves,"
Henry said.

Just then, Henry knocked
brown paint all over
his painting!

Henry tried to cover the brown paint with blue paint, but that made a big, muddy mess!

"Oh no!" cried Henry.

"We can come up
with a plan,"
Angelina said.

"What else do you love to do?" she asked.

"Well, I love to explore and climb mountains," said Henry.

"We can change the waves
into mountains,"
Angelina said.

Angelina and Henry
worked together
to fix the painting.

"Now I am climbing a big mountain!" Henry said.

Soon, it was the day of the Chipping Cheddar Art Fair.

"Henry, I really like your
painting!" Alice said.